For Georgia:
artist, kitten healer, friend
–A.L.V.

For Nick
–L.F. & S.J.

With My Hands

Poems About Making Things

Words by Amy Ludwig VanDerwater

Pictures by Lou Fancher & Steve Johnson

CLARION BOOKS • Houghton Mifflin Harcourt • Boston New York

CLARION BOOKS

3 Park Avenue, New York, New York 10016

Text copyright © 2018 by Amy Ludwig VanDerwater

Illustrations copyright © 2018 by Lou Fancher & Steve Johnson

Clarion Books is an imprint of
Houghton Mifflin Harcourt Publishing Company.

hmhco.com

The art was rendered in acrylic, crayon, ink, colored pencil, and collage/cut paper.
The text was set in Bazhanov.
Book design by Sharismar Rodriguez

Library of Congress Cataloging-in-Publication Data
Names: VanDerwater, Amy Ludwig, author.
Title: With my hands : poems about making things /
Amy Ludwig VanDerwater ; illustrated by Lou Fancher & Steve Johnson.
Description: New York : Clarion Books, Houghton Mifflin Harcourt, [2018]
Identifiers: LCCN 2017010266 | ISBN 9780544313408 (hardcover)
Classification: LCC PS3622.A5947 A6 2018 | DDC 811/.6—dc23
LC record available at https://lccn.loc.gov/2017010266

Manufactured in China
SCP 10 9 8 7 6 5 4 3 2 1
4500692310

Maker

I am a maker.

I am making
something new
with my hands
my head
my heart.

That's what makers do.

A maker starts with
empty space
ideas
hope
and stuff.

A maker
pushes
through mistakes.
A maker
must be tough.

A maker is
a tinkerer.
A maker will
explore.

A maker creates
something new
that
never
was
before.

Painting

When it's my turn at the easel
I love standing there
staring at an empty paper
making pictures out of air.
I can mix bright blue with yellow.
See! I mixed light green.
I can build a world with color
no one's ever seen.

I can paint a horse.
I can paint the moon.
I can paint a daisy in a vase.
I can paint designs.
I can paint a car.
I can paint my mother's face.

Painting makes me giggle on the inside.
Nobody can tell me that I'm painting wrong.
Painting!
How I love to paint!
I will paint my whole life long.

Clay

Hold a lump of clay.
What does it want to be?
Make a coil.
Pinch it.
Roll it.
Listen.
Set it free.
You will hear it tell you
what it is
what it is not.
And you will know
if you should shape
a puffin
or a pot.

Birdhouse

We hammered out
a little house.
It has a circle door
four sturdy walls
a pointed roof
a simple wooden floor.

It's hanging on
a fence post
and I'm imagining
a bluebird mom
in there
with babies
tucked beneath
her wing.

Someday
I'll see them fly.
Someday
I'll hear them sing.

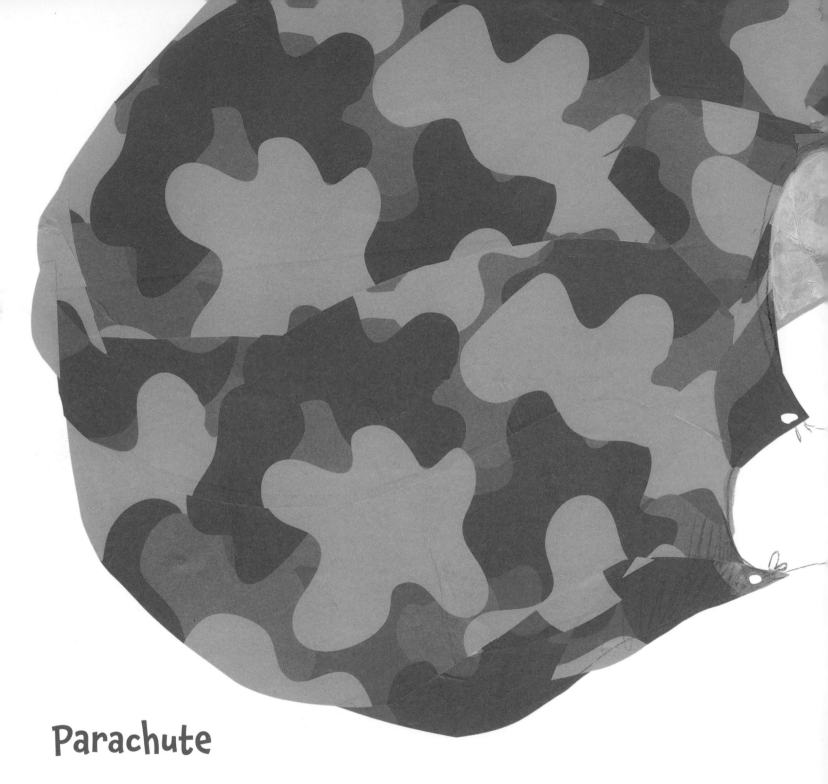

Parachute

I cut a parachute from plastic
tied my guy on with elastic
threw him from a window (drastic)
watched him drift to earth—fantastic!

Boat

Today I made
a little boat
from twigs and foil
so it can float.
I named
my homemade boat
The Wish.
Inside
it bobs
with rubber ducks.
Outside
it races fish.

Card

I picked out a card.
It said *Number One Dad!*

I thought it was perfect
but then I felt bad
about picking a card
from a stack in a store.
No dad is like mine.

So I walked out the door.

I went home to my crayons
my scissors
my glue.
I cut and I wrote.
I thought and I drew.

Happy Father's Day, Daddy.
I made this for you.

Knot

This knot
is not easy to tie.
It is not.

You showed me.
I listened.
I've tried it a lot.

Is this right?
It's not tight.
Over.
Through.
Wrap it.
Under.
Around.
Back again.

I am starting
to wonder—
Will I ever learn
to tie puzzles
in rope?

I am knot giving up.
I can do it.
(I hope!)

Soap Carving

A whale hides in this bar of soap.
I'm carving with my plastic knife
a little here, a little there
so I can bring the whale to life.

Curl by curl
from head to tail
I carve away what is not whale
and as fresh soap falls
flake by flake
I know it's whale
I'm meant to make.

My two hands swim in endless motion.
My brain dives deep beneath the ocean.
Carefully I carve a spout.
Bit by bit
the whale peeks out.

I'm carving with my plastic knife
a little there, a little here.
If I keep working, I am sure
my hands will make the whale appear.

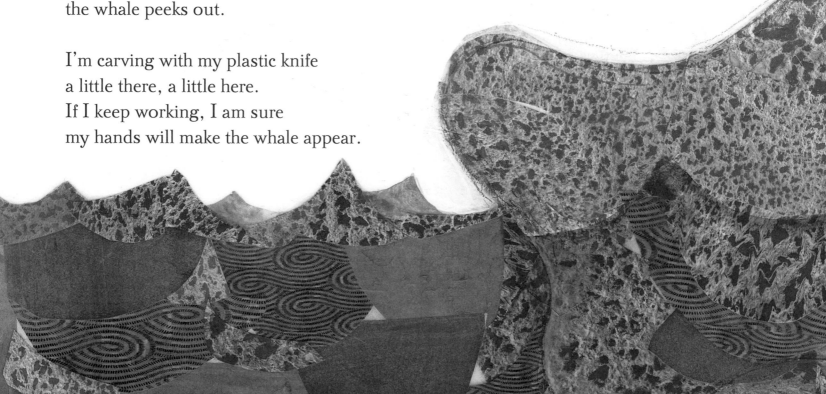

Tie-Dye Shirt

I made a tie dye.
Didn't buy it.
Twisted.
Tied it.
Dipped it.
Dyed it.
Rinsed.
Untied it.
Shook it.
Dried it.
Wore it.

Try it!

Collage

This
kaleidoscope
of scraps
torn from
tattered
photographs
is a window
to my heart
showing
everything
I love.

Piñata

I have mixed a flour glue.
I have ripped up bits of news.
We can make a big piñata.
We can make two if we choose.

But first come help me dip each paper
in a bowl of gloppy paste
one by one. It's sloppy. Careful!
Don't let any go to waste.

Lay each gooey strip of paper
onto this big red balloon.
We don't want to miss a spot.
We can take all afternoon.

Next we'll dry our wet piñata.
Paint it yellow like the sun.
Dry it. Cut a hole to fill it.
Hang it. Now we're almost done.

Our sun is swinging from a pine tree.
You are spinning through the air.
Blindfolded, you smack it squarely.
Quick! There's candy everywhere!

Glitter Picture

Shiny   speckles

     flashing   freckles

tiny   blinking

      treasure-twinkles

  shower   from   my   shaker

     in a   starry   stream

    of   winking   sprinkles

drizzle   on   my   picture

   in   a   glinting   glowing   gust

as   I   sing   and   scatter   glitter

dazzled   by   its   diamond   dust.

Mess

Yes. It's my mess.
Do not let it distress you. ·

I'm making a project
that just might impress you.

Projects are messy—
all makers agree.

And the messiest maker
of projects is . . . me.

Spaceship

I built the spaceship on this box.
It looked just like the picture said.

But then I pulled it back apart
to make the one that's in my head.

I see spaceships every day
rocketing inside my mind.

I would rather build those ships
than make the one this box assigned.

fins

hot

turbo blaster

toss
Follow the Directions

hot

Wear a helmet

nose cone

hot

Sock Puppet

If I were a sock
I'd long to be
a puppet
who could
speak and see.

But socks can't say
the way they feel
for socks can't talk
through toe or heel.

So I will sew
a face that's fine
as cute as yours
as cute as mine
clipping felt
to make a nose
sewing lips
on woolen toes.

I hope my sock
will realize
I'm the one
who gave him eyes.

Drawing

I learn to draw by watching.
I learn to draw from books.
I pay attention to my life.
I notice how it looks.

When I see a spider
I do not hurry past.
I pull out paper, pencil.
I sketch quietly, and fast.

I learn to draw by staying still.
I follow every line.
I love to draw because I know—
what I draw is mine.

Leaf Pictures

When maples tossed
love letters
onto the ground
we gathered them up
and threw them around.

We whistled and walked
on the edge of our road
stuffing leaves
into pockets
till they overflowed.

We brought them all home
laid them
this way and that
on long sheets of wax paper.
We ironed them flat.

Our leaves look like
stained glass—
pointy and pretty.
They help us remember
fall
    in
        our
            city.

Fort

Make one out of fuzzy blankets.
Make one out of fallen sticks.
Make one out of packing snow.
Make one out of mud and bricks.
Make one in your bedroom closet.
Make one out of anything.
Make a pillow fort in winter.
Make a flower fort in spring.
Make some walls with furniture.
Make a squishy, mossy floor.
Make a window out of ice.
Make a secret hidden door.
Make a little box for mail.
Make a path from river stone.
Make whatever kind you wish.
Make a fort to call your own.

Origami

I gently tear
just as I'm told
one perfect square
I neatly fold
inside and out
so I can hold
a polar bear.
(It's almost cold.)

Cookies

You're not even looking
but you know
we have been cooking
for we're filling
up the kitchen
with a smell
of something good.
We are stirring
hands aflutter
mixer whirring
eggs and butter.
We resemble
clouds of flour
(as two
busy bakers should).
And these goodies
we are making
were a batter.
Now they're baking
into cookies.
Will you help us
eat them up?

We knew you would.

Snowman

I roll and stack
my snowman
whisper-white
and fat.

I give him
one red
one blue eye
a carrot nose
my cowboy hat.

At last I say
You're looking good.
His rock teeth
form a grin.

I hug a mug
of cocoa
with my hands
when I go in.

Knitting

My grandma taught me
how to knit
and when it's cold
I like to sit
with needles
and a ball of yarn.
I think of sheep
out in a barn
wearing wool
that soon will be
knitted by
someone like me.
And as my fingers
twisty-twirl
each stitch into
a knit or purl
I watch my window
fill with snow.
I listen
as my needles go
clicking-clacking
to and fro
and watch
my knitting
grow
and grow.

Snowflakes

I love snipping snowflakes out of paper.
I could snip all day.
Folding snipping hearts and circles
is for me the perfect way
to spend a Sunday afternoon.
New shapes flitter to the floor.
I snip and clip in symmetry
snipping folding
snipping more.

Sometimes I sit and snip and think
my flakes of paper piling high
snipping looking out my window
watching snow fall from the sky
and wish
that I could meet the girl
who snips real snowflakes out of white.
Her scissors must be very small.
Her dancing hands snip through the night.

Shadow Show

When birds are snuggled into nests
when night begins to fall
my hands like making shadows
in the spaces on my wall.

The moon peeks in my window
like a knowing, glowing eye
to help my hands turn into birds
and flapping fingers, fly.

My hands are dogs and dragons
for I learn new shapes each night.
Shadow-shapes of cats and trees
dance through moony light.

My hands like telling stories
of forest, sky, and sea
whenever we play shadow show
my wall, the moon, and me.

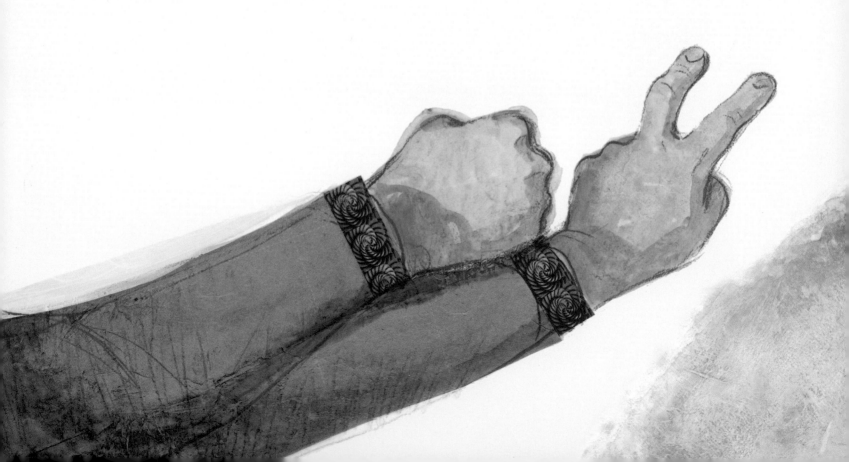

With My Hands

When I make something new
I am never the same.

I can never go back
to the person I was.

For the thing that I made
is a part of me now.

I changed it.
It changed me.

I am different
because

I brought a new something
to life with my hands.

If you are a maker
then you understand.